MISS MELINDA MANNERS

Story by: Celia Danielle Frances
Illustrations by: Katy Jackson

In Dedication:
To my family who raised me to be neat and tidy
To my children who give me the motivation to write,
be concise, and stay whimsical
To my friends who nourished my growth and success
To my past and present students whom I will always adore
To authors that wrote books I have enjoyed and continue to enjoy
Finally, to my husband who encouraged me when I was discouraged
and pushed me to make this dream of mine come true
I could not have done it without you.
Thank you.

Miss Melinda Manners lives in a fluffy cloud
and loves to help families on the Earth's ground.
In her pin striped bows and polka dot dress,
she is always neat and never a mess.
Her hair is straight and her cheeks light pink;
her smile is bright, and she sparkles
when she winks.

She is best at cleaning and entertaining too and is always sure to say "please" and "thank you." Because a polite fairy is always a success, Melinda Manners comes to help those in distress.

"Hello, I am Miss Melinda Manners, and I get called, when children's manners are not being used at all. I come to your home to teach you a fact: there is a right way a person should act."

It just so happened one morning around breakfast time a bright girl named Lily started to whine.

"Mommyyyyy, I want breakfast with peanut butter and fluff!
Do not give me any of that green healthy stuff!
I want my princess plate with my pirate cup,
and I do not care if it is not clean enough!

I want my fruit punch and my candy roll!
I want it now, not later - I want it all!"

"Now that I'm up, I won't make my bed,
I won't get dressed in what you've said.
I want to watch TV and my iPad too,
going to school is NOT what I want to do!"

Lily's tantrum went on as her bus drove away, an hour went by, and she continued to fuss in this argumentative way.

Lily kicked, stomped, and yelled so loud
that her voice reached Miss Melinda Manners' cloud.
Without hesitation the fairy came to Earth's ground,
to see who was making all those noisy sounds.

"Excuse me, I say, when I interrupt-
I flew here to tell you enough is enough. Miss Melinda Manners is my name, and I am going to teach you a game."

"We will start from the beginning and take it real slow to make sure you learn what you need to know."

Lily was stunned to see a fairy appear, so she
listened to her voice which was sweet and clear:
"It is hard to wake up early, I will agree,
but let's try something new, you and me."

"Let's lay out clothing from the night before,
something appropriate you like and adore.
Set your alarm with some time to spare,
so you have extra time to fix your hair."

Lily listened and set out for her drawers, she picked out her favorite top and shorts.
She programmed her alarm to 6:15, and by herself made her bed look pristine.

Miss Manners glowed and Lily grew excited—
What else could Miss Manners do when delighted?

"Dear Lily," said the fairy, "onto the next. Here is an important word called Respect: Whenever you have a wish or desire, go over to the person you are speaking with and gently inquire:

'Please may I have something of my choice,'—and make sure you are using a soft indoor voice. You may not be given a YES right away, but your family will be pleased you asked the courteous way."

Lily shrugged and thought about this,
"My mom doesn't listen when I pound with my fists.
A tantrum is never okay, she insists.
It doesn't work when I scream and shout because...
that is not what being polite is all about."

"A question I have, if I may, what if I want something right away?
I surely do not like to wait all day!"

Miss Melinda Manners responded with a smile,
"Keep in mind if you do not get what you care for,
it is okay because your family may have other things in store.

A 'thank you' should follow with a nice sweet smile, and they will be happy that you went the extra mile."

Miss Melinda Manners twirled around.
Her sparkles flew from the sky to the ground.
Her polka dots perked up and her bow gleamed bright pink,
then Miss Melinda Manners gave a magic wink...

She watched as Lily, without delay, apologized to her mom in a respectable way.

"I am sorry mom, I tantrum so much, I do not like it when I am in a rush.
Miss Manners taught me how to prepare for school, so I will not act like I am entering a duel."

Mrs. Nono smiled. "Lily, my dear, it is time to eat. What would you like? - I will make you a special treat."

Lily thought for a moment and then spoke up:
"May I please have a peanut butter sandwich made my way, with fluff, my princess plate, and my pirate cup?"

Mother replied, "Your voice was calm and your manners so kind.
A sandwich made your way? I do not mind.
One extra thing I must declare,
a veggie on your plate is only fair..."

Lily listened and politely agreed.
"I must ask nicely for the things that I need. Thank you, mom, I see my voice was too loud, next time I will be quieter, act nicer, and make you proud."

Mrs. Nono was filled with glee,
to see that her daughter was as polite as can be.

Miss Melinda Manners, Lily, and Mrs. Nono all sat down and ate lunch together before Miss Manners flew back to her cloud.

With a polite thank you and a kiss goodbye, Miss Melinda Manners was very satisfied!

DISCUSSION PAGE:
(Miss Melinda Manners' Message):

Speaking in a calm and polite voice is really important...

When is it okay to whisper? yell?

How many times did you say "please" and "thank you" today?

How do you get ready for school in the morning?

Do you prepare from the night before?

CPSIA information can be obtained
at www.ICGtesting.com
Printed in the USA
BVHW020035251019
562019BV00003B/14/P